TALES OF
A DEAD KING

TALES OF
A DEAD KING

WALTER DEAN MYERS

14607

WILLIAM MORROW AND COMPANY
New York | 1983

84 · 127746

1   2   3   4   5   6   7   8   9   10

Library of Congress Cataloging in Publication Data
Myers, Walter Dean, 1937–   Tales of a dead king. Summary: Two American
teenagers uncover a plot to rob the tomb of an Egyptian pharoah. [1. Mystery and
detective   stories.   2.   Archaeology—Fiction.   3.   Egypt—Fiction]   I.   Title.
PZ7.M992Tal   1983   [Fic]   83-5373
ISBN 0-688-02413-0

To Joyce

I awoke a half hour before we were to land in Cairo. The stewardess gave me a glass of orange juice and said that I looked as if I had slept well. Actually, it had taken me a long time to fall asleep. It wasn't so much the fact that sitting up all night in an airplane wasn't the most comfortable way to spend the eight hours the flight had taken, as it was the excitement of going to Egypt for the first time.

Six months earlier, my father had read a small

news item about a girl in New Jersey named Karen Lacey who had been selected from among five hundred high school students to go to Egypt on an archeological dig. The competition had been sponsored by the university that was supporting the research. The most interesting part was the name of the Egyptologist who was leading the dig, Dr. Erich Leonhardt. Leonhardt was my mother's maiden name and Dad remembered her once mentioning that someone in her family was an archeologist. We couldn't wait for her to get home from shopping.

"Well, there's no picture of him but it has to be my uncle Erich." Mom still had her coat on as she looked at the newspaper article. "We didn't see a lot of him as kids; he was always off in some exotic part of the world teaching or digging. My father used to say that he was the odd one of the family. He used to have this very shy smile. I liked him as a child, and when I got older I used to think that he just needed someone to be kind to him.

"He would stay with us for a week or so and then he would be off again. The last we heard from him he was teaching somewhere in the Middle East."

That just about made the conversation for that evening until my father turned to me and asked how I would like to go to Egypt, too.

"If he's letting one student go with him he might as well take a second," Dad said, "especially if it's his niece's son."

2

I had always been interested in archeology and the chance to go to Egypt was like a dream come true. I told Dad I'd love to go.

Mom wrote Dr. Leonhardt a letter and three weeks later we received a reply from Aswan, Egypt. He said that he would be glad to have me come on the first of August and looked forward to seeing me. He also said that the way things were turning out he could use all the help he could get. That's how I found myself trying to clear the cobwebs out of my head and looking for my shoes in an airplane four thousand miles from home.

The airport at Cairo wasn't nearly the size of the one in New York, but I still had a hard time finding my way around. A thin brown man selling sodas directed me to the flight that connected with Aswan. I had my luggage checked by customs and the airport security people, then I sat in the waiting area. The airport was interesting. Men in jellabas, the long robelike things that I had seen in so many pictures of the Middle East, were more common than men in western-style business suits. I would have liked to have wandered outside to see if I could see anything of Cairo but decided against it.

Finally it was time to board the plane and, after having my passport checked for the third time since I had arrived in Egypt, I boarded. It was a smaller plane this time and many of the dark men I thought to be Egyptians stretched out and went to sleep.

The flight from Cairo to Aswan took less than

two hours, and I found myself in the smallest airport I had ever seen. There was a small building that might have been a terminal, but it was closed and we were told to wait near it for our baggage. There were a few taxis and the drivers came up to the handful of people waiting for baggage and offered their services. The airport was dark except for two small lights on the corner of the building, and I was getting just a bit nervous.

"Excuse me." The voice startled me and I must have jumped a little.

"Oh, hello," I said. She looked as if she could have been an American and about my age.

"I'm Karen Lacey," she said. "I noticed you on the plane. You wouldn't, by any chance, be . . ."

"John Robie," I said, extending my hand. "I'm pleased to meet you. Are there others on the plane who are headed for the dig?"

"We're the only ones," she said. "My father called Dr. Leonhardt about a week ago to find out how many were going. If you weren't going I would have had to skip it."

She looked like a nice person. She was pretty, almost as tall as I was, and perky. While we waited for the bags we talked about Egypt and about going on a dig. I was a little disappointed to find out that she had gone on a dig in Texas and knew more about them than I did.

"There's not a lot to know about them," she said. "You just have to do what you're told. That's proba-

4

bly more important than anything else, but they're fun."

"I guess I'll manage," I said.

Some men pulled over a skidload of bags and started placing them in a row on the ground. I found my two, and Karen lugged over four and put them next to mine. I couldn't imagine what she'd have in four bags.

Dr. Leonhardt's letter said he had arranged a room for me at the Grand Hotel. Karen had the same arrangements so we shared a cab.

I was exhausted by the time the smiling driver had packed our bags into the trunk and back of his car and squeezed us into the front. We couldn't see a thing as we left the airport. Aswan wasn't much of a city, that was for sure. It took us nearly twenty minutes to reach the Grand Hotel. If the Grand Hotel was anything, it wasn't grand.

"*This* is where we're staying?" Karen looked at me and her eyes grew wide.

"Well, if this is near a dig it's probably not that close to the city," I said.

I was trying to be reassuring but I wasn't feeling very reassured myself. The Grand Hotel was on a wide street that was paved in most places, but there were large patches of dirt. The hotel itself looked like one of those old saloon hotels that you see in Westerns, only instead of cowboys hanging around the lobby and Miss Kitty or somebody playing the piano, there were two guys in hoods sitting on a

5

beat-up sofa that sagged on one side. We split the cab bill, which came to four Egyptian dollars, and lugged our bags to what passed for a front desk. An old guy in a business suit two sizes too big for him looked up slowly from his newspaper and asked us, in perfect English, what we wanted. This was a relief because the cabdriver had talked to us all the way from the airport and I hadn't understood more than two words he had said.

"I'm Karen Lacey. Is this the *only* Grand Hotel in Aswan?" Karen asked the desk clerk.

"How many Grand Hotels can there be in one place?" he asked. He took off his glasses and held them up to the light. He saw that they were dirty, wiped them off on his sleeve, and put them back on. "You have a reservation?"

"I think so," I said.

He looked at me closely, then leaned over the desk and looked at my shoes. Then he took a ledger from under the desk and went through the names.

"Miss Karen Lacey from America?"

"That's right," Karen said. I thought she looked disappointed that the clerk found her name in the book.

"I'm John Robie," I said.

He went back to the first page and went through all the names again until he found mine a few listings under Karen's. He gave us our room keys and called two black boys over to help us with our bags.

The kid that took mine looked too skinny to be carrying two bags but I figured he must be stronger than he looked. He wasn't. The bags nearly killed him and I had to help him up the stairs. The stairs, because the elevator didn't work.

Our rooms were on the same floor and Karen gave me a weak smile before she entered hers.

At best the room was a disappointment. A dim lightbulb dangled on a long chain suspended from the middle of the high ceiling. There was a closet against one wall. Against the other, between the shuttered windows, was a low chest on which sat a tin ashtray and a putrid green plastic doily that vaguely matched the wallpaper. But far and away the most striking feature of the room was the presence of five single beds lined up less than a foot apart, facing the door. It looked like a place where they would give you a bowl of soup and a New Testament in the morning.

I gave the kid that brought my bags up a dollar and closed the door. The lock didn't look as if it was meant to keep anybody out.

I opened my bag, took out the letter from Dr. Leonhardt, and read it again. There was no mistake; he had said the Grand.

I thought about going over and knocking on Karen's door to see what her room was like, but decided not to. I figured if she didn't mind her room, I'd put up with this one.

I selected the bed farthest from the door after checking to make sure that the bolt was latched. I checked the sheets and they seemed clean enough. I switched mental gears the best I could and told myself that I didn't mind the shabbiness of the hotel at all. I had just settled into the lumpy bed when I thought I heard a voice coming from the bathroom. My heart just about stopped cold. I sat up in bed and listened. Nothing.

I got up and went into the bathroom, holding my breath. There was a light string dangling from the high ceiling and I pulled it. I looked around the bathroom, but it was empty. Then I heard the voice again and figured out where it was coming from. The top of the wall next to the bathtub had a square opening. I heard water running and guessed that the bathroom next to mine didn't have a window, so they were ventilating it through my bathroom. It was too high, a good ten to twelve feet high, to look over, but it provided some air for the inner room and you had the pleasure of hearing whoever it was next door take a shower. Beautiful.

It was 6 A.M. Egyptian time when I got back into bed. I fell asleep quickly. I woke up with a start when I heard a rapping on the door. The room looked as dismal by daylight as it had by the dim overhead bulb three hours before. I quickly slipped into my pants and shirt and went to let Karen into my room.

"I have *never*," she was sputtering as she talked, "in my entire life seen—what are you doing with five beds?"

"Beats me," I said. "I think they didn't have wall-to-wall carpeting so they threw in a few extra beds."

"This is the dumpiest place I've ever stayed in," she said. "Why on earth would Dr. Leonhardt pick a place like this?"

"I don't know," I said, "maybe it's the only hotel in Aswan."

"No way," Karen said. "I heard the taxi drivers asking what hotel the others were going to. And there's no way that I'll believe he picked this because it's the best one."

"Well, I guess the dig is the important thing," I said.

"Yeah, sure," Karen watched as I tied my shoes. "Come on, let's find our good doctor and get this show on the road."

I persuaded Karen that it would be a good idea if I washed my face before going downstairs. Seeing how ticked off she was at the hotel amused me a little.

The same desk clerk, wearing the same oversized suit, was talking on the phone when we got downstairs. When we went to the desk, he turned away from us and took his own sweet time about finishing his conversation. Karen bet me that Dr. Leonhardt was staying someplace else. I took the bet.

"You're looking for Dr. Leonhardt?" the clerk asked.

"We're going to be working with him," Karen said.

"He's my great-uncle," I said. I didn't have to turn my head to feel Karen giving me a look. "He's my grandfather's brother."

"You?" The clerk pointed his finger in the general direction of my nose.

"Yes," I said. "I really don't know him though."

"He's your relative?" He pushed his glasses up on his nose. For once he looked interested. "I see . . . I see. Look, why don't you go in and have some breakfast. I'll see if I can locate him for you."

Breakfast sounded fine to me but Karen wanted to take a look around in the daylight. We stepped outside into a brilliant morning sun. There were already a number of people on the street. An old truck lumbered toward us, belching puffs of black smoke, then stopped as a dog meandered into its path. The black driver leaned out the window and railed at the dog in some language that the dog seemed to understand. The dog barked back and continued his trip across the wide steet. There were horse carriages parked along the far side of the street. A small group of men were seated on a low bench, some of them sipping from cups. I took them to be the drivers of the carriages.

The street itself was dusty. But on the far side the

earth was green. There was a stand of trees in front of me on the other side of the street and beyond them the Nile shimmered gently in the clear morning air. A hundred yards from where Karen and I were standing there was a large boat that could have been a steamer. Moored next to it was a row of sailboats, some with colored sails that lay slack against the tall masts. There were boats on the water as well, their white sails billowing with the gentle breeze as they gracefully glided over the smooth water. The river, nestled in the lush greenery, was as beautiful as the Grand was ugly.

Karen and I crossed the street and looked closer at the river we had both heard so much about. Some guys that looked about my age, but darker than most of the other Egyptians we had seen, tried to get us to take a ride on what they called feluccas. I remembered having heard the name before. From being fairly upset over the hotel we found that the Nile really changed our mood. I was even tempted to try a ride on one of the feluccas when we heard the clerk from the hotel calling us.

"Leonhardt must have shown up," I said.

The clerk made a sweeping bow to us as we went back into the Grand.

"Here they are," the clerk announced. "Arrest them!"

The uniformed man was about my height, which is five ten, but twice as broad. The guy he had with him was shorter and didn't look very formidable

11

except for the machine gun he had slung over his shoulder. That looked pretty formidable.

"You are Mr. Robie?" The police officer looked me over carefully.

"Yes."

"And Miss Lacey?"

"Yes, is there anything wrong?"

"I am Captain Gamael. Perhaps we can have a word or two?"

He said it nicely, but I had a sneaky feeling that he wasn't about to take no for an answer. We went into the dining room, and Karen and I had coffee with the captain while the guy with the machine gun slouched in the doorway.

"What business do you have with Dr. Leonhardt?" Captain Gamael asked. The small cup of coffee looked like a toy in his huge hands.

"May I ask why we are being questioned?" Karen asked. She had her snippy voice on again.

"I am just curious," Captain Gamael said.

"Well, I'm curious as to why you're curious," Karen said.

"The reason I mention my curiosity," Gamael said slowly, "is because when I am only curious I don't have to go through the bother of arresting you. Egyptians like to keep things simple. Do you know what I mean?"

We did. We explained how we had come to Egypt in the first place and what we were going to be doing. Captain Gamael listened very carefully. He had our passports, which we had given to the desk clerk, and he looked at them carefully, too.

"This Dr. Leonhardt, he's a brilliant man?" he asked.

"I guess so," I said. "I'm his grandnephew, but I don't really know him. You know what I mean?"

"No," he answered. "How can you belong to the same family and not know each other?"

"Well, we live in Michigan, and he lives . . . somewhere else." It sounded a little lame.

"Do you know where he is now?"

"The desk clerk said he'd try to find out," Karen said.

"Well, there is some problem," Captain Gamael spoke slowly. "Dr. Leonhardt *was* staying here, but then last week he suddenly disappeared. He didn't pay his bill. One day he was here and the next he was gone. Don't you think this is strange?"

"You mean he's just . . .?" Karen looked at me and I shrugged.

"He left his notebook and a few old clothes, that's all," Gamael said. "Mr. Mahdou, the owner of the hotel, is very disappointed that such a distinguished man would leave without even saying goodbye."

"We're disappointed, too," I said.

"How long will you be in Aswan?" Captain Gamael asked.

13

"I'll be out of here as soon as I can book a passage," Karen said.

"Why don't you stay a few days to see the sights, since you are here," the policeman said. "Perhaps sail in a felucca."

Captain Gamael shook our hands gravely, returned our passports, and left. I looked at Karen and couldn't think of a thing to say. We had traveled halfway around the world to dig up mysteries of the past, and here we were stopped cold by a modern mystery.

Karen was packing within ten minutes, but I didn't know what I wanted to do. The money my folks had spent was mostly for the roundtrip air fare. That was going to be spent no matter what I did. The hotel wasn't much, but it was paid for three weeks in advance. There was a travel agency, Wagon Lit, near the hotel, and I went there and talked to one of the agents. He said that I couldn't normally change the airline tickets, but since it was a special circumstance they might let me and bill my father for the difference. What I decided to do was nothing.

"You're just going to hang around here?" Karen asked. "That's dumb."

"Look, maybe he's just like . . . you know, an absent-minded professor or something," I said. "Maybe he left for a week or so and then he'll come back."

"And maybe he won't."

"Besides, he's my mother's uncle and . . ."

"So what?" Karen said. "You don't even know him."

"In a way I do," I said. "I have this picture of him looking a little like my mother, probably tall because my grandfather was tall."

"But you don't really *know* him," Karen said.

"Right, and he doesn't really *know* me," I said, "but he let me come along on the dig. Or at least it seemed that he intended to before . . ."

"Before what?"

"I don't know," I said, "but I think I could at least try to find out."

"I guess you're right. Maybe I'll stay around a few days, too," Karen said. "But this great-uncle of yours had better show up pretty fast."

We decided to look around Aswan a bit. The guy at the travel agency had been pretty friendly so I went and spoke to him, and he told us that we could get someone to drive us around to see the sights in a few hours.

"There aren't too many sights in Aswan," he said, "but the ones that are here are nice."

There turned out to be a lot to see and I enjoyed the tour, especially the unfinished obelisk, the great dam and the temple of Philae, which we reached by taking a motorboat to an island about a mile from Aswan. Under any other circumstances it would

15

have been great, and I tried hard to enjoy myself. But I could see Karen was uptight.

The hotel lobby looked gloomier than ever when we returned, but we had already told Mr. Mahdou we were staying.

"Mr. Robie," Mr. Mahdou called to me just as I reached the steps—the elevator hadn't worked for nearly a year, if it ever had—and I went over to see what he wanted. Karen leaned against the railing of the circular stairway and watched as I prepared myself for another question-and-answer period.

"Dr. Leonhardt left some papers with me for safekeeping," Mr. Mahdou said. "Do you want them?"

I didn't know what to say. I didn't have any right to his papers, really. And what would I do if he didn't show up again? I was just about to say no when Karen brushed by me.

"Yes," she said. "We'll take the papers."

I could tell that Mr. Mahdou would rather have given them to me, but he handed them over to Karen anyway.

They weren't papers, really, but notebooks. I was fairly excited about having them and, when Karen just turned and walked away, I stopped to thank Mr. Mahdou.

"The point is," Karen said, answering my questions before I could ask them, "he knows where you live in the States and he can simply write to us if

16

and when he shows up again if he wants them back."

That made sense, a lot of sense, but I didn't tell Karen that. I mean, she was really bright, but I didn't like the way she just took charge of things.

"You want to take a look at the notebooks now?" I asked, hoping she would say yes.

"Let's wait until later," she said. "It'll give us something to do in the evening."

I said okay, even though I was disappointed. I went to my room and Karen went to hers. I had just taken my shoes off and was brushing the sand off my socks when I heard a scream in the hallway. I held my breath. It couldn't have been Karen, I told myself. A moment later there was a frantic pounding on my door.

"There's a snake on my bed!"

Karen was white as a sheet and gasping for breath. I pulled her into my room and went across to hers. The door was ajar and I walked in cautiously, looking on the floor in front of me before taking even the smallest step. I was halfway across the room when I saw it, twisted in the bed sheets. It must have been an easy three feet long and brown with yellow markings. The head was covered and I thought there might be just the oustide chance that it wasn't really a snake. I got enough courage from somewhere to go to the edge of the bed and pull the sheet off. It was a snake. It didn't move and I

17

thought that it might have been asleep. I wasn't about to wake it up and ask if it hadn't made a mistake in its room number. I went back to my own room where Karen waited in the middle of the floor.

"It's a snake, all right," I said.

"I told you that," she said. "Now what are you going to do about it?"

"I'll get the owner," I said. There was no way I was going to touch that bugger.

Mr. Mahdou wasn't there. A young girl was in his place and she called over one of the guys that doubled as porters and waiters in the dining room. She said something to him in Egyptian, and he looked at me with a disbelieving grin.

"I follow you, my friend," he said.

It took a flat two minutes to get up the three flights. The porter kept looking at me and smiling all the time, which annoyed the heck out of me. When we got to the room he motioned me in first and I stepped inside and pointed to the snake. His eyes bugged out and he said something in Arabic. Then he left. A few minutes later he returned with two other porters and Mr. Mahdou. They all gathered around the bed and one of the porters poked at the snake with a stick. It took them about ten minutes more before they were convinced that the reptile was dead.

Karen insisted that her room be searched

18

thoroughly before she would enter it. I even helped, although I wasn't too energetic about it. I figured that at least it would be something to tell my folks when I got home, which I thought would be pretty soon. When Mr. Mahdou and his searchers had left, shaking their heads, I thought I would find Karen packing again. As usual, I was wrong.

"You mean you're going to stay?" I asked.

"I said I would stay," she said, her arms folded over her chest, "and I will. For a few days, at least."

I wasn't that anxious to stay any longer myself. My father and mother warned me not to expect too much, but what they had meant was that perhaps Dr. Leonhardt wouldn't involve us too much in the dig, that we wouldn't learn much. They hadn't considered the possibility that he wouldn't be there at all, or that we might have to share our beds with snakes, dead or otherwise.

When we finally calmed down, we went for dinner and Mr. Mahdou told us that the meal was on the house, which made me feel pretty good.

"He probably told the snake the same thing," Karen said.

"You think he had something to do with it?" I asked.

"Who knows?"

"After dinner, maybe we can go through Dr. Leonhardt's notebooks," I said. "Maybe we'll find some reason he had to leave."

"There's nothing that I can see," she said.

"What?"

"Well, I had to do something while you were looking for snakes," she said. "You can look at the notebooks yourself if you want."

I didn't say a word for the rest of the dinner. I went up with her when we had finished eating and looked under the bed while she stood in the doorway. Then she had me open all of her drawers and the closet to check for snakes. I was so ticked off at her looking through the notebooks without me, after she had made such a big deal of waiting to look at them together, that I wasn't even nervous.

"You really get mad easily, don't you?" she said as I left.

I did a quick check around my room for snakes, just in case, and settled in with the notebooks. There were three of them, two almost completely filled while the last one had only two pages completed.

What was in the notebooks was familiar to me. It was the story of how Howard Carter had discovered the tomb of King Tutankhamun in 1922. I had read many accounts of it and had seen the Tutankhamun exhibition when it came to the States. The funny thing was it read as if Carter was writing the diary, as if it were happening now, instead of over sixty years ago! I read the last page over and over again:

All that is needed now is C's approval and we can begin to unearth the last great mystery of the period. Each day I wait for the post to arrive to see if final approval has been realized.

I recalled the story of how Tutankhamun's tomb had been discovered by Howard Carter under the sponsorship of Lord Carnarvon, and how he had waited for Lord Carnarvon's arrival in Luxor before actually opening the tomb. I began to wonder if Dr. Leonhardt had been poking around in old tombs a bit too long and had gone off the deep end.

I'd been interested in archeology ever since I saw the Tutankhamun exhibition. When I found out that I was going to Egypt on a real dig, I read everything I could get my hands on about Egypt and the explorations. I couldn't understand why Dr. Leonhardt was so interested in Tutankhamun's tomb. I was sure that it didn't make sense to Karen, either. I went over the last few pages again before going to sleep.

In the morning I knocked on Karen's door but there was no answer. The thought came to me that we had overlooked one of the snakes and that I would find Karen's body lying in the middle of the floor. First I had an image of the entire room with her body on the floor, then I saw a close-up of her throat with two tiny puncture marks. I tried the knob and was glad the door was locked. I wasn't too anxious to be the one to discover the body.

I hurried downstairs and was on my way to the front desk when, glancing into the restaurant, I spotted Karen. She was there having breakfast. So much for the Curse of the Serpent.

"Good morning," I said, trying to sound cheerful. She was still the only person I knew in Egypt.

"What," she asked, holding up a slice of ripe tomato on her fork, "do you think of male chauvinist pigs?"

"Well, I don't like them," I said. I mean, what are you supposed to say to something like that?

"I see," she said.

I got the feeling that I was going to be zapped the way she'd zapped me with the notebooks.

"Our friend Mr. Mahdou has a letter and he won't give it to me," she said. "I'm sure it's purely because I'm a woman. What do you think?"

"Could be," I said. What I thought was hurrah for Mr. Mahdou.

She didn't say anything more, and the waiter came over and asked if I wanted an American or Egyptian breakfast. I figured Karen must have had the Egyptian breakfast because the only thing I recognized was the tomato. I said I'd have the American breakfast.

Karen didn't say a word during breakfast. I knew I was supposed to ask about the letter so she could finish her zapping but I didn't. Finally, she broke down.

"Aren't you curious about the letter?" she asked.

"Why should I be curious about a letter addressed to you?" I said.

"It's not addressed to me," she said. "It's addressed to you, but since Mr. Mahdou *knows* we're traveling together . . ."

I found Mr. Mahdou and got the letter. It had to be from either my parents or Dr. Leonhardt.

I went outside and across the avenue to the bank of the Nile. There were benches there and I found one that wasn't occupied. A driver of one of the horse carriages parked across the street from the hotel came over to me and asked if I wanted to go to the market.

"No," I said, anxious to get to the letter.

"Two American dollars for one hour," he offered.

I smiled and said no, and he smiled and said two dollars for an hour and a half. I smiled and said no again and he shrugged and left. By that time Karen had found me.

She didn't say anything. She just sat at the other end of the bench and watched me. It was going to be a long-distance zap.

The letter was postmarked Khartoum, which is in the Sudan, the country south of Egypt. It was from Dr. Leonhardt.

Dear John Robie and Karen Lacey:

I am quite sorry about the trouble I have undoubtedly put you through. I have been called away to Khartoum on urgent archeological business to which I must attend. From here I will most likely get the *S.S. Sibuna* to England where I will complete my monumental work.

I hope sincerely that you understand why I have had to disappoint you.

Dr. Erich Leonhardt

The opportunity of going on a dig had been the biggest thrill of my life. The letter from Dr. Leonhardt was the biggest letdown.

Karen shook her head in disbelief as she read the letter herself. She started to say something to me, stopped, and then got up and walked slowly back toward the hotel. I watched her stop and look again at the letter before entering the hotel.

I felt hurt and disappointed. On the Nile a steamer chugged along. There were birds following it, diving into its wake for the bits of fish caught up in its screws. I thought about calling my parents, but I just wasn't up to it yet. Maybe the next day, I thought.

When I got back to the hotel, Karen was in the lobby talking with Captain Gamael. She was crying, but more out of anger than sadness.

"I want to call the United States Embassy!" she was saying. She had been in the hotel for only ten minutes or so before I got there, and I wondered what was going on.

Captain Gamael was rubbing a small stone between his fingers. He motioned for me to have a seat next to Karen. The letter from Dr. Leonhardt was on the bench next to him.

"It's an interesting letter that you received," Captain Gamael said.

I looked over to where Mr. Mahdou was sitting and he looked down at his newspapers. He must have called Captain Gamael as soon as he received the letter.

"Why do you think Dr. Leonhardt would write to you and not write to Mr. Mahdou to pay his hotel bill?" Captain Gamael didn't take his eyes from mine as he spoke. "It's not all that much he owes."

"I don't know," I said.

"He says that he will sail on the *Sibuna*, but I have called the police in Khartoum and they don't know of such a ship."

"Well we certainly don't know anything about what ships sail from Khartoum," Karen said.

"When he wrote to you in America, did he mention an Ahmed Khattab?"

"No," I said. "Not to me, anyway."

"Me either," Karen said. "Who is he?"

"Someone who worked for him," Captain Gamael said, "and also someone to whom he owes a little money. Just one more question," Captain Gamael said, standing. He handed me the letter from Dr. Leonhardt. "Why do you suppose he did not put his return address in Khartoum on the letter?"

"Because he was going to England," Karen said.

"Ah, that explains it," Captain Gamael said. "I hope you both will enjoy your stay in Aswan."

"Fat chance!" Karen muttered.

We watched as Captain Gamael nodded to Mr. Mahdou and left.

"I'm packing now and getting out of here on anything that flies, rolls, or crawls!" Karen said. She started clumping up the stairs in front of me just in case anyone missed the fact that she was mad. "They're questioning us as if we're common criminals or something! I'm so mad I could spit!"

We got to our floor and she stormed into her room, slamming the door even harder than I expected.

I went into my room, lay across the bed, and tried to think things through. From time to time I reread the letter, but it still didn't make any sense. Mom had said that her uncle had always been the odd one of the family. Well, this was certainly odd. On the other hand neither Captain Gamael nor Mr. Mahdou had mentioned anything about Dr. Leonhardt acting strangely before he disappeared.

I thought of going to sleep but it was still the middle of the day. I found myself sitting at the window looking out over the Nile. The scene that had looked so beautiful before, almost like a picture postcard with moving parts, now seemed dreary.

I remembered some of the things I had read about the Nile. Farther north, toward lower Egypt, in Luxor, there had been a legend that the Nile separated the living from the dead. That on one side of the river the living held sway and on the other side was the province of the spirit world. There was something about that legend, or about Egyptian mythology, that bothered me. I worked at it for another few minutes, but I couldn't quite put my finger on it.

I was torn between moping in my room by myself or trying to find Karen and moping with her. I was halfway between the two when I picked up the letter and reread it for what must have been the twentieth time. Suddenly a piece of the puzzle clicked into place. It was like having a large jigsaw puzzle and suddenly two pieces of clear blue sky fit together. I didn't know what it meant or if it meant anything, but it was too strange to be a coincidence. I went and knocked on Karen's door.

"I'm just finished packing," she said.

"Look," I said. "Captain Gamael found out that there wasn't any ship called *Sibuna*, right?"

"Yeah."

"I guess he also figured out that *Sibuna* spelled backwards is Anubis?"

"Anubis?" She picked up a pencil and wrote it on an envelope. "A-N-U-B-I-S—Anubis, the Egyptian god of the underworld. What are you trying to say?" she asked.

"Me? Nothing," I said. "What's Dr. Leonhardt trying to tell us?"

We took the letter down to Mr. Mahdou, who as usual was reading his newspaper. Karen showed him the letter, the reference to Sibuna, and that it spelled Anubis backwards.

"It's got to mean something!" Karen said.

Mr. Mahdou looked at the letter carefully, held it up to the light, and even wrote Sibuna backwards on the desk. Then, after what seemed forever, he took his glasses off and looked up at us.

"So?"

"So?" Karen's voice went up in pitch.

"So he lies about where he is now," Mr. Mahdou said, "the same way he lies about paying his bill and about meeting you here. You want me to give this letter to Captain Gamael again and show him what two great American minds can come up with?"

"I think not," I said, taking the letter.

We stopped outside Karen's door. I was back down in the dumps and I thought Karen would be, too. When I looked at her she was rubbing her nose with the palm of her hand and I thought she was trying to keep from crying. I didn't blame her.

"Go on and cry if you want," I said. "I feel about the same way."

"Who's crying? I'm thinking about that letter. Doesn't it strike you as being a bit odd?"

28

"You mean that bit about Anubis?" I asked.

"Not that so much as the fact that he sent a letter in the first place. He knew we were coming. If he was really sorry about missing us he could have left word for us before he took off instead of leaving us hanging."

"The letter wasn't very encouraging," I said. "Maybe he just didn't want us hanging around here."

"I think someone doesn't want us hanging around here," Karen said. "But they won't get rid of me that easily."

"Wait a minute," I started to protest as she put the key in the lock. "What are you going to do? You just can't hang around and . . . and . . ."

"And find out where Dr. Leonhardt is?" Karen asked. "Why can't I? I'll just treat it as a modern archeological problem. Anyway, if I get the run-around from somebody I want to at least know why."

I was glad that Karen was going to stay. I think if she had left I would have too. But I sure didn't want to.

I spent the rest of the afternoon walking around Aswan, taking pictures and buying souvenirs to take home. Karen didn't want to go along, and I didn't really mind that much. I went to her room later, though, and we had dinner in the hotel restaurant together.

That evening I was lying on one of my five beds

telling myself how hot it was and how many flies there were and how Karen and I weren't going to find out anything about Dr. Leonhardt if Captain Gamael couldn't, when I finally thought of something smart to do. I got up, grabbed a handful of Egyptian money and left the room. I went quietly through the hall, so as not to disturb Karen.

The Egyptian night was hot and sultry; what breeze there was came at me like a blast from a hot-air heater. In front of the hotel, a cabdriver lolled against the battered fender of a Volvo that had seen better days. I got in and waited for him to snap out of his lethargy and slip behind the driver's wheel.

"The Cataract Hotel," I said.

There were really two Cataract Hotels, the one with a lot of charm and high ceilings, and the new Cataract, a stone's throw away with what I guess passed for plastic charm and ceilings low enough for even me to slam dunk. But what the new Cataract did have, or at least I had heard that it did, were decent telephones.

I asked the operator for a long-distance line, then gave the long-distance operator the number I wanted. After a number of whirls, clicks and soft whistles I heard a familiar voice.

"Hello, Mom? This is John."

"You're calling all the way from Egypt? Is everything all right?"

30

"Well I'm over here all right," I said. "But your uncle isn't."

"What happened?" she asked.

"Beats me," I said. "They say he just left."

I heard her calling for my father to get on the other phone.

"Hi, son, how's it going?" My father was shouting into the phone.

"Kind of strange," I said. "We got over here and Dr. Leonhardt had left the hotel already. We got a letter from him from Khartoum saying he was sorry, but I think the letter's a little weird. He said he was sailing to England on the *Sibuna.* You know what that is backwards?"

"What *what* is backwards?" my mother asked.

"Sibuna."

"What's a Sibuna?" Mom asked.

"It's Anubis backwards, that's the Egyptian god of the underworld."

"That's nice." This from Mom.

"Let me get this straight," Dad said. "You got to the right place? You're sure of that?"

"They even know Dr. Leonhardt over here," I said.

"And he wasn't there?"

"Right."

"And he wrote you a letter that said what?"

"He was sorry, he got called away, and that we should just go home."

31

"But he thinks there's something wrong with the letter," Mom said. "Isn't that right, John?"

"Sounds like a mix-up of some sort," Dad said. "What are you going to do now?"

"I don't know. What do you think?" I asked.

"How's your money holding up?"

"Fine."

"Why don't you go back to Cairo and see the pyramids," Dad said. "Since you're over there and all."

"Oh, okay."

"Look, John, are you worried? I mean are you upset about this whole thing?"

"No, not that much, I guess. It's just a little strange."

"Life is like that, son. If things didn't go right, though, you might as well take advantage of being over there."

"Sure."

"If you have any problems, go to the American Embassy," Dad went on.

"And if you feel sick, go to the hospital right away," Mom said.

"Why should he feel sick?" Dad asked.

"They have some strange diseases over there," Mom said. "You know that's Africa."

"He's not going to be sick, don't worry about it. There's a Hilton in Cairo and he'll be fine there."

"How about Uncle Erich, do you think you'll hear from him?" Mom asked.

"I think I'll look around a little, see if I can locate him," I said.

"John, that's sweet of you."

"Take pictures, son," Dad said.

"And call if anything goes wrong, you hear?"

"Yes, Mom."

"He'll be okay," Dad said.

We said our goodbyes and I grabbed a cab back to the Grand. I felt a lot better about staying in Egypt. I fell asleep easily.

When I woke I felt a slight breeze. There was also the sound of music in my room. I took a breath and opened my eyes slowly. The music was coming from the other side of the room. I sat up, hopefully with a look on my face that didn't show how I felt, and saw Karen having breakfast at my table.

"What are you doing in my room?" I asked, relieved.

"I knocked twice and you didn't answer," she said, stuffing toast into her mouth. "So I jiggled the knob a couple of times and it opened. I brought you up something but you took so long waking I ate it."

"What's the music?"

"Portable radio. I thought you'd want to get an early start if you were headed back home. There's a flight at eleven to Cairo if you want."

"I've decided to stay," I said. "Sometimes when I get a question like this gnawing at me, it bothers me for weeks. I might as well get to the bottom of this before I go home."

"And your folks won't mind?"

"Sometimes you have to do things on your own, Karen," I said. "You can't depend on your folks being around to wipe your nose every minute."

"My father's a football coach and my mom's a designer," Karen said. "They won't start worrying about me until their seasons are over. Anyway, I might have come up with something else."

"Oh?"

"I checked the watermark on the paper the letter was written on," she said. "It was made by an Egyptian company. He could have picked it up here and taken it to Khartoum, but I doubt it."

"Why?"

"Because the paper he wrote me on had his name and title printed on it. That's probably the paper he normally uses. It's expensive paper, not the kind you would leave behind. So, for some reason, our Dr. Leonhardt probably had to leave in a bigger hurry than he would have liked."

I was almost glad the dig didn't come off. Karen would have made me look like an idiot. I pulled the blanket around myself and went into the john where my clothes were. I took a slow shower while I mentally went over everything that had happened. The only thing that I came up with was the reassuring fact that it had been me who had noticed that Sibuna spelled backwards was Anubis. Just in case, I went over a few other words in my mind, spelling them backwards, but nothing else came.

"So what do you think we should do next?" Karen asked.

"Beats me," I said. "You seem to be the junior detective on the case."

"An archeologist is a detective of sorts. I thought you were interested in the field?"

"I am," I said, weakly. I made an instant decision to switch my act to the strong silent type.

"Didn't Captain Gamael ask us if we knew somebody?" Karen asked. "An Ahmed somebody?"

"I think it was something like that. But we don't know where he is."

"No, but Captain Gamael does."

"Sure," I said, "but you just can't walk up to him and ask him."

▲　▲　▲

"Why do you want to find Ahmed Khattab?" Captain Gamael's office was large and nearly empty except for his desk, which was in the middle of the room, and another small desk in the far corner. "You said Dr. Leonhardt had not written to you of him?"

"No," Karen spoke up first, as usual. "But you mentioned him, and since we're going to spend a few days looking for Dr. Leonhardt, we thought we might talk to him."

Nothing. That's what Captain Gamael said and I figured he didn't believe a word we were saying. He just sat there and looked at us, first at Karen and then at me, for a long time. After about a minute of this, I didn't believe a word we were saying either.

Finally he reached into a drawer, pulled out some papers, and started looking through them. I noticed that his eyes were the same color as his skin, a very light brown. "I can find out for you, perhaps, where he is working. Do you want me to do this thing?"

"Yes," I said, beating Karen to the lip for once.

Captain Gamael shook his head and, taking the paper, left the office. We could hear his footsteps as he walked down the long hall that we had come up when we went to his office.

"I'll look out for him," Karen said. "You look through the papers on his desk."

Uh-oh. A quick trip to terror city. Karen was standing in the doorway, acting as if she were looking at the woodwork, and motioning like crazy to me to start looking through the papers. A vision of me drawn and quartered by four camels came to mind.

"Get up!" Karen hissed. "Are you chicken or something?"

"Yes!" I hissed back.

"You don't have to touch them, just look!" She said in a hoarse whisper.

Against my better judgment, I went around to the other side of the desk and looked at the top letter. I was so scared I could hardly read it. It was from the University of Chicago and addressed to

Dr. Leonhardt. I went over it once without understanding a word I was reading and then again after taking a deep breath.

"Here he comes!"

Karen came running back and I jumped around the edge of the desk, or almost around because I nearly knocked my knee off on the corner trying to get to my chair, which Karen had already plopped in. I took a big step over her, my knee gave way completely, and I landed with a thud on the floor between the two chairs as Captain Gamael came in. Although in truth, I just thought it was Captain Gamael. I couldn't see him through the tears. Then I knew it was him as he came over to me and spoke in that quiet way he has.

"You don't find the chairs comfortable?"

"I have a bad back," I said. "Sometimes I have to sit on the floor."

"I can tell by your face that it must be quite a painful condition," he said, returning to his seat.

I started to get up but he said it was all right, that he didn't mind me sitting on the floor.

"Did you find where Khattab works?" Karen asked.

"I'm afraid not," Captain Gamael said. "He works here and there as he finds jobs. You know jobs here are not easy to come by. Sometimes he works in the markets, sometimes he works as a laborer. But he is Nubian, as are most of the felucca boys. Why don't you ask them, eh? If you find something interesting, maybe you tell me, all right?"

"Yes, we will," Karen said. She was standing, so I got up. I tried to leave Captain Gamael's office without limping, but it wasn't easy.

We got a cab back to the Grand and I moaned all the way. I hobbled up to my room while Karen got some ice. She was being very friendly but I knew it was just because she wanted to know what was in the letter. I also knew that as soon as I told her what was in it she would think it through in about two minutes and know more than I. So I pretended the knee hurt even more than it did while I tried to put it all together myself. When I finally settled on the bed with an ice pack on my knee, I told her that I still felt badly and had to have a Coke to settle my stomach. When she said that she didn't think it would help, I pretended to get sick, and she went out for the Cokes.

The letter hadn't seemed worth a bruised knee to me. What it boiled down to was that Dr. Leonhardt had asked for something from the University of Chicago.

Karen got back with the Cokes, opened one for me, and sat on the edge of the bed.

"Well?"

"The letter said that the University of Chicago went along with somebody else's recommendation," I said. "Apparently they were saying no to Dr. Leonhardt about something."

"When was it dated?"

"The letter?"

"Of course."

The only of course was that of course I forgot to look at the date. I told her and she made this face like "how could I be so stupid."

"I wonder if Chicago could be the *C* he meant," Karen said.

"What *C*?"

"Remember in his notebook at the end when he said something about all we need is *C*'s approval or something like that?"

I hobbled out of bed, got the notebook, and looked at the last page. Sure enough, there it was: "All that is needed now is *C*'s approval and we can begin to unearth the last great mystery of the period."

"I thought the *C* stood for Lord Carnarvon, the guy who was in charge of the Tutankhamun expedition," I said. "Or he could be talking about something else altogether. The letter from the university said they didn't think that the tomb of Akhenaton could be found that far from the Valley of the Kings, right?"

Karen was rubbing her nose again. "Most of the tombs they found in the Valley of the Kings, right?"

"Go on."

"And they didn't find Tutankhamun's tomb until 1922 because it was under another tomb, which was why it wasn't looted."

"Yeah?"

"Yeah? What more do you want?"

"How about telling me where Dr. Leonhardt is?"

"How about finding out what he was working on when he left in such a big hurry," Karen said. "Then maybe I can tell you where he went."

"I'll tell you what happened," I said. "First the money for the dig was cancelled. That's what the letter from the University of Chicago was all about. Then he thought about getting some volunteers—"

"Like us."

"Then he got discouraged and just left. Right now he's probably somewhere drinking tea and thinking of his next project."

"You believe that?"

"Not really," I said. My knee was really beginning to ache. "But I can't think of anything else. I'm going to take a walk before this knee stiffens up."

Karen was rubbing her nose, and I finally broke the code. When she rubbed her nose she had an idea, when she scratched it she didn't.

I left Karen sitting on my bed and started for the door.

"John," she called after me, "what do you know about Akhenaton's life?"

"There isn't a lot to know," I said. "He believed in one supreme god, which made him unpopular in a land with so many gods. They found a tomb he had built, but they don't know if he was ever actually buried in it. They didn't even find his mummy."

"Anything else?" She followed me out of the room.

"They think his mother was Nubian," I said, starting down the stairs.

"Aren't the Nubians from around here?" Her voice came through the yellowed slats of the bannister.

I stopped on the staircase. The girl could think her way through a brick wall. I could see what she was driving at, though. Maybe Leonhardt had found something around here that made him think that Akhenaton was buried nearby. Karen was rubbing her nose again.

"So?"

"So you want me to come with you?"

"So come on," I said.

"The way I see it," Karen was saying as we walked slowly down the street toward where the cruise boats were docked, "Dr. Leonhardt must have thought that Akhenaton's tomb was somewhere around here and that's what he was working on. Then the money fell through, or something else happened, and he disappeared."

"Or maybe he's playing PAC-MAN in London," I said.

"Don't you think that guy's headpiece is a nice green?"

41

Karen was looking toward an Egyptian looking into one of the shop windows.

To me green is green. I don't like one more than the next. But I figured that as smart as she was, Karen was probably interested in clothes, as most girls are.

"Lovely," I said. "I'm going to get one just like it."

"Don't be so silly!"

"Can we get back to what we were discussing?" I said.

"Oh, all right. Let's suppose that Leonhardt did find Akhenaton's tomb. If the tomb had been looted, what kinds of things would be in it?"

"The others had gold and jewels and . . . Wow!"

"Wow is right," Karen said. "If anyone got wind of what he was working on before he had a chance to report his findings—"

"You mean he might have found Akhenaton's tomb and then . . . somebody found him? We'd better try to find the tomb ourselves," I said.

"How, is the question."

"Didn't Captain Gamael say that Ahmed was a Nubian? I wonder . . ."

"Are you really going to get one of those cute green hats?" she asked.

"You know," I said, "it really takes a girl to start talking about how cute a hat is in the middle of a discussion in which somebody's life could be in danger!"

That shut her up for a while. It wasn't that I didn't like her, because I did. I just hated to have to tag along behind somebody that switched back and forth from being superbright, which was a pain, to talking about the color of somebody's dirty hat.

"You want to get something to eat?" she asked. "We can stop at one of the places on the water."

We had walked past the large cruise boats docked along the banks of the Nile. The top decks were usually half full of people who would wave if you looked at them. The restaurants along the water's edge, which were like the greasy spoons in a factory section of town, were usually half full too.

We went into a small restaurant called the Cleopatra and ordered shish kebab and sodas. Watching the Nile had a good effect on me. It made me feel cooler and peaceful at the same time.

"I still like that green," Karen said. "Do you think it's Nile green? I mean we're so near the Nile and everything."

I was about to lose my temper, stopped, and turned to where Karen had been looking a moment before. He sat on what remained of a concrete wall, pretending for all the world to be lost in thought, his long robe wrapped about his legs, his green headpiece covering half his face. We were being followed!

I turned back to Karen who was smiling over her shish kebab.

Being followed was a lot of fun, like watching the

dentist putting black marks on your chart to mark the cavities. But I was cool.

"The thing to figure out," I said calmly, "is what exactly does this guy want."

"There's no use lowering your voice," Karen said. "He can't possibly hear us from here. Anyway, I think the thing to figure out is whether or not he wants to kill us or something."

So much for cool. Karen finished her meal and the remainder of mine and we tried as best we could to casually walk out. Something clicked in my mind and I had a vague memory of having seen a green hat before. He had been around the hotel, I remembered, when we first arrived. He could have been the one who put the snake in Karen's bed. But I figured that he probably didn't want to kill us. The snake in Karen's bed had been dead and she was too young to have a heart attack from fright or something. The doors to the hotel rooms weren't that secure. If anyone had wanted to get us they would have already. I hoped.

"If this guy is following us—and I'm sure he is," I said, "there must be a reason. We don't have anything worth taking, so it's got to have something to do with Dr. Leonhardt."

"Very clever," Karen said. I didn't think she really meant it, though.

There wasn't any use going back to the hotel, so we decided to take a ride on one of the feluccas

44

while we still had some daylight. The feluccas were beautiful, exceedingly graceful boats. For a couple of dollars you spend a leisurely hour or so sailing up the Nile. It was also a chance to find out more about Ahmed Khattab. Captain Gamael had said we should ask the felucca boys about Ahmed, so we went over to the boats, fended off a few of the young Nubians who didn't speak English well, and then engaged a young Nubian dressed in a red-and-white caftan.

The water seemed perfectly still and there was no wind at all as Yusef, the young man we engaged, pushed away from the dock. The Nubians were a deep black color with regular features, gleaming white teeth, and curly black hair. Yusef moved about the boat quickly, turning it toward the distant cataracts and rigging the one sail at the same time. I watched him standing at the rear of the boat, the rudder between his thin, dark legs, his hands adjusting the lines, and wondered how his life was different from mine. We must have been close to the same age. I looked at Karen as she sat on the flat cushions that Yusef had provided, her eyes almost closed. But then she rubbed her nose and I knew she wasn't sleeping. She was thinking again.

We had settled in and had been traveling a good fifteen minutes with Yusef, making polite small talk, when Karen spoke up.

"Do you know a man named Ahmed?" she asked.

Yusef grinned broadly. Then he looked at his hands and started counting on his fingers.

"I have four Ahmeds in my family," he said, holding up four fingers. "And in my uncle's family there are three."

"Ahmed Khattab," Karen said. "I think he does odd jobs."

"Ahmed Khattab?" Yusef raised his hand to show a tall person.

"I don't know," I said. "But he used to work with the doctor at the hotel."

"Ah, yes," Yusef smiled and nodded. "Now he is working at the theater. He sells sodas and drinks. You know the theater?"

We didn't, of course, and we couldn't make heads or tails of Yusef's directions. I thought we might as well make the most of the felucca ride and stretched out the best I could.

Sailing down the Nile was a glorious experience. On the banks there were women washing clothes as they must have for thousands of years. Farther down two men were cooling off a water buffalo who was covered with water up to his horns. It was as if I was in a time warp. The Nile, which twisted through the very center of Egyptian life, couldn't have changed very much. The people along its banks, some robed much the way they would have been hundreds, even thousands, of years ago, probably still lived in much the same way as they always had.

"A penny for your thoughts," Karen moved nearer to me.

"Oh, just imagining myself as a pharoah sailing down the old Nile. You can fan me with a palm leaf if you like."

"Don't hold your breath," Karen said.

"What were you thinking?" I asked.

Karen started going on about some movie she had seen where everybody who had been connected with some pharoah's tomb had died a horrible death within two years.

Great. I shut Karen out and watched some children playing along the shore. A kingfisher hovered for a moment and then dove into the water, coming up a moment later with a fish in its beak. A white ibis posed solemnly on a rock as if he was waiting for someone to take his graduation picture. I kept thinking about the guy in the green hat and telling myself that there was no reason in the world for anyone to want to hurt a nice girl like Karen, let alone a nice fellow like myself.

We sailed past Elephantine Island and down to a small Nubian village before Yusef turned the boat around. We had to tack into the wind and the boat dipped close to the water.

"If you would like to go to some of the other islands, I can take you tomorrow," Yusef said, when I had paid him.

"Maybe," I said. It was the kind of life I could grow into easily.

Karen nudged me on the way back to the hotel. She didn't have to. I had seen Green Hat from the moment we landed.

Yusef had said that there were evening dance performances at the theater and we checked at the hotel desk. The girl who replaced Mr. Mahdou in the evenings didn't know anything about the dances. Karen went into the dining room, and I told her to order for me while I went next door to the travel agency. I found out that the program was mostly of Nubian ethnic dances. I made arrangements for Karen and me to be picked up at eight that night.

"How do you know that I want to go?" Karen asked.

"So don't go," I said.

"Did you know they dance and have parties down here almost every night?" she asked.

I had seen a lot of young people in the Grand. The clientele was a mixture of teenagers in designer jeans, guys with robes, one or two in business suits, and, oh, yes, one dead snake.

"You want to go dancing?" Karen asked.

"I'm more interested in what's happening with Dr. Leonhardt and perhaps trying to learn a little more about life in this part of the world," I said.

"You mean you can't dance, either?" she asked.

There was a radio on somewhere outside of the dining room and she began to bounce her head to the beat. If I had found a dead snake I knew just where I would put it.

I thought she would go to the theater anyway, but she didn't. The guy from Wagon Lit picked me up on schedule and bought a ticket for me. Inside the theater wasn't much. One side of the curtain was lower than the other and it was badly faded. I sat on the first floor, near the front. Most of the people around me seemed like Egyptians with one or two obvious tourist-types interspersed. The weather was warm, but some of the Egyptian women were wearing fur coats. I guess there wasn't a lot to do in Aswan in the evenings.

Most of the noise came from the balcony. I looked up and saw that the people in the balcony were very dark and probably Nubians.

The Nubian dancers were really good. Their dancing told stories, one or two of which were explained in English and then in French by a young girl. I soon forgot about Dr. Leonhardt and about Karen as I was caught up in the music and dancing. It was a free and graceful performance for the most part, and I enjoyed it.

After the show I hung around until I spotted some people who were cleaning the theater. I asked two of them if they knew an Ahmed before I found one that spoke English.

"Ahmed? Him." He pointed to a guy going down the aisle collecting bottles.

49

I went over and asked him if he was Ahmed Khattab.

"Yes," he said. "Are you the man who brings me my fortune?"

"What fortune?" I asked.

"You don't have a fortune for Ahmed?"

"No."

"Pity. It would make you feel so good to make me happy," he said, picking up another bottle from between seats. "And it would make me feel so good to be happy."

He went on down the aisle as I watched him. He was big, well over six feet tall, and muscular. His face was round and shiny, like a black moon; his narrow eyes made his head look even bigger than it was.

"I understand you knew Dr. Leonhardt," I said.

He looked at me and then turned back to his bottles.

"I'm trying to find out what happened to him," I said.

"This white man you are talking about is not an honorable person," Ahmed said. "I worked for him and he didn't pay me. He steals my wages from me. One day he is here, the next day he is gone. Did you come to bring my wages?"

"No," I said.

"You are rich?"

"No, not at all," I said. I was hoping I looked poor.

50

"Then your father is rich," Ahmed announced. "How many American dollars did it cost for you to come over here?"

"About two thousand," I said, knowing what was coming next.

"Then the poor must do very well in your country, sir."

"John," I held out my hand. "John Robie."

His hand was so big that it felt like I was a kid shaking hands with his father. I went on to tell him about how Karen and I had come to Aswan looking for Dr. Leonhardt and how he had disappeared. I told him about Karen and about being questioned by Captain Gamael, but I didn't mention Green Hat or the dead snake.

Ahmed just kept looking at me, shifting from one foot to the other, sizing me up. When I had finished he just turned and went on looking for bottles. For the first time I wished I had the Lip with me. Karen would have thought of something to say.

"You wouldn't want to meet my friend Karen, would you?" I asked.

"She bring me my wages?" Ahmed asked.

"No," I said, "but if we can find Dr. Leonhardt, we can ask him about your wages."

He seemed to think about this for a moment, and so I told him that we could all have breakfast together in the hotel the next morning if he wanted to. He said no, to meet him at the theater at "maybe ten, maybe eleven." That was as close to a

51

firm time as I could get him so I left. I found a cab outside the theater and got back to the hotel.

I went to my room and found Karen sleeping on my bed.

"Karen," I called gently, then shook her by the shoulder. I looked at the night table and saw a bottle of Coke, half empty. I didn't know the girl would take my being away for just one night so hard.

"How was the show?" she asked.

"Okay," I answered. I had left the door open and went over and closed it. "I liked it a lot. I found Ahmed, too."

"Hey, that's great," she said.

"I'm not sure if it's great, but I think he'll be useful," I said.

"I danced with some guys from Switzerland and some from Cairo," Karen said. "They're a little wild. One insisted on walking me to my room. I told him he couldn't come in because my husband wouldn't like it. He stood at the top of the steps as I knocked on the door."

"Who answered?" I asked.

"While I knocked with one hand I jiggled the lock with the other hand until the door opened. I also found out something about Green Hat. When you left by taxi I was watching from the window. Green Hat came out of the shadows near the hotel the moment the taxi pulled away. He stepped out into the street to see where the taxi was going.

Then he looked up toward your window. I didn't want to stay here by myself so I went down to the lobby. I saw him in one of the booths making a phone call."

"You think he's working with somebody in the hotel?"

"I don't know," Karen said. "I just know he gives me the creeps."

"He doesn't scare me as much as something else," I said. "Like what they might have done to Dr. Leonhardt." I drew my finger across my throat. "I'm going to talk to Ahmed again. He was pretty sore about not getting paid. He seemed as annoyed as we were that Leonhardt had disappeared. I told him that we'd meet him tomorrow at the theater."

"Okay, we'll do that."

"Hey, Karen, you don't have to, you know."

"I know. But when I'm not scared to death with this thing, I'm so curious I could bust," she said. "You going to walk me to my room?"

"To keep you from mugging somebody along the way?"

I walked Karen back to her room and she gave me a friendly punch on the arm. I went back to my room, locked the door from the outside, and tried to open it by jiggling the antiquated lock. Nothing. I opened it with the key and went in. As I lay in the dark I wondered about Karen following Green Hat. On the one hand it could have all been accidental;

53

she didn't want to go to the theater with me, saw
him checking out the cab, and went downstairs. On
the other hand, she could have planned to let me go
off to see if he would follow me. Then, again, where
had I been when Dr. Leonhardt disappeared? My
paranoia was really working overtime.

▲   ▲   ▲

"All I know is that the man is gone and so is my
money," Ahmed was dressed in a gleaming white
caftan. "He owes me for two days work."

"What were you doing for him?" Karen asked.

"I do everything for him," Ahmed said. "When
he first came to Aswan, he asked me to take him to
my village. I took him there. He listened to all the
old men's stories about a Nubian King who was
buried someplace around here. He want to go dig, I
go dig with him."

"Where did you dig?" I asked.

"We dig here and throw the sand around,"
Ahmed pointed to a spot near his feet. "Then we go
over there and dig and throw the sand around.
Then we get in the car and go someplace else and
dig and throw the sand around. Sometimes we dig
in the sun so hot it fries your brain. Then we come
out and dig at night."

"You find anything?" Karen asked.

"One time Dr. Leonhardt say he found something pretty important. Then we get into the car
and race like crazy for the hotel."

"When did you last see him?" I asked.

"I took him to see my friend Kwami in the market," Ahmed said. "From Kwami you can buy anything."

"What did Dr. Leonhardt buy?"

"I don't know," Ahmed said. "I had another job so I went to it, and Dr. Leonhardt said he would meet me at the hotel in the morning. I went to the hotel, but no Dr. Leonhardt. I have not seen him since."

"Maybe this Kwami can tell us something," Karen said.

"The police have already spoken to him," Ahmed said.

"Right, but I haven't," she said.

"I don't think we can get any information that Captain Gamael couldn't," I said.

"Then don't come with me," Karen said.

Most of Aswan was relatively uncrowded. The wars in the Middle East had cut down on tourism. The market, on the other hand, was something else again. What it amounted to was wall-to-wall people, mostly black or brown, equally divided between native and western dress. We followed Ahmed's pace through the crowd; he'd pause only to exchange cross words with someone he'd brushed against or whose donkey had splashed water on him.

It was like walking through some place where they were testing all of your senses. There would be a place where they sold gaily colored fabrics, and then a spice shop with its pungent aroma, or an incense shop filled with thin wisps of smoke from the burning incense and an unbelievable amount of strange odors.

Ahmed stopped in front of a small shop. The windows were filled with brass plates and ornaments displayed against a deep-red rug. Sitting outside, an incredibly thin old man, his black head covered with hair that had greyed unevenly, puffed contently on a hookah set down beside him. Ahmed spoke with him in Nubian in a voice so low I could hardly hear them. Then he turned to us.

"He says that the captain has already spoken to him," Ahmed said. "He doesn't know anything more than he has said."

"Ask him what Dr. Leonhardt bought," Karen asked.

Kwami said something to Ahmed and then went into his shop.

"He says Dr. Leonhardt bought something but didn't take it with him. He still has it inside."

We followed Ahmed into the store. Inside there were more brass items and some souvenir-type things. There was a bench against the far wall and Kwami opened one of its drawers. There must have been at least a dozen watches, cameras, knives, and even a few calculators. Kwami took a package from the drawer and opened it. It was filled with serving spoons, large forks, and other things that you would use for cooking.

"Well?" I looked at Karen.

"It makes sense if he was setting up a house somewhere," she said. "He'd need something to cook with."

Karen screamed as the sudden clatter of metal against metal jerked us from our thoughts. Two brass pots came tumbling down to the floor and a row of ornamental dishes followed. I hit the floor and covered my head with one hand. I looked up for Ahmed and Kwami and saw the old man cowering in the corner. Ahmed was against a far wall on his hands and knees. He had both arms over his head. Very reassuring.

We stayed like that until Ahmed got up and went to the door. He looked out cautiously. I was still kneeling and got a view through his legs. People outside were looking in. The way my knees were shaking it was an effort to stand up.

"What was that!?" Karen asked.

"Someone threw that through the door," Ahmed said.

I looked to where he was pointing. It was a curved dagger, over a foot long, stuck into a wooden beam.

Kwami was yelling in Nubian and trying to push us out of the door.

If there were ever a time to hop into a telephone

booth and shed my mild-mannered appearance, it had come.

"Somebody's trying to kill us!" Karen screamed.

I gave her an easy smile and took deep breaths so I wouldn't throw up. All the while Ahmed was looking around wild-eyed and letting out a kind of half growl. Outside the sun was as hot as ever. The only thing different was that all the mild-mannered shoppers in their long caftans had turned sinister, their faces half hidden in the shadows of their hoods. I didn't see any green hats.

Ahmed pointed in the direction of our hotel, and we made tracks for it.

By the time we got to the Grand I needed a Coke and I needed it bad. We bought four in the lobby and took them to my room. We checked it carefully for snakes, tarantulas, black mambas, and anything else the fiends might have hidden.

"I figure if we get the plane from Aswan, we'll reach Cairo in time for dinner," I said. "If they still want to kill us I want them at least to have to pay the air fare to reach us."

"Why?" Karen asked.

"Why?" I thought she might be going into hysterics. "Because I don't want to die at somebody's convenience, that's why."

"No, why do you want to leave Aswan?" she said.

"Because I'm not ready to kick the breathing habit."

"That's what they want you to think," Karen

said, rubbing her nose. "They want us to *think* that somebody's trying to kill us."

"I'm easy to convince," I said. "Put one snake in my bed and throw one dagger at me, and I'm a believer."

"Think about it," she said. "It was a dead snake. If they wanted to kill me—and it was my bed not yours, they put the thing in—they would have used a live snake and I'd be dead by now. Someone threw a knife into the store, which means two things. That we were being followed and that they wanted to scare us. Whoever threw the knife could probably have hit us if he had wanted to. I don't think we have a thing to worry about.

"Another thing," Karen went on. "Those cooking tools. I think that Dr. Leonhardt is somewhere around here. If he's moved into a private apartment then he'd need that kind of stuff."

"I still think you're crazy," I said. "It could have been an old snake who had a heart attack, and maybe the guy who threw the knife was shaky."

"Could be," Karen said. "But if we don't know anything about where Dr. Leonhardt is . . ."

"And we don't . . ."

"Then why would anyone want to kill us?"

"How's this for openers?" I said. "Up until now we were sticking fairly close to the hotel and just guessing at what happened. Now we've contacted Ahmed and this Kwami character. We could be getting a little too close."

59

"But no closer than Captain Gamael," she said. "So there must be something that somebody thinks we'll find out that Captain Gamael doesn't know."

"There was one thing. You remember in the letter—that bit about his 'monumental work'?" I said.

"Go ahead."

"Well, at first I thought he was just blowing his own horn a little and that bothered me because my mom was saying that he wasn't that kind of guy. But he might have said that if he had lived in Aswan three thousand years ago. This is where they got the granite to make the monuments. The unfinished obelisk is an example of it. They would quarry the granite here, then float it up the Nile to Egypt."

Karen clapped her hands. "So if he was going to maintain proximity to the materials for his 'monumental work,' he'd still have to be around Aswan some place."

"Right."

"So why didn't you say that before?"

"I didn't think of it before," I said. "You think that maybe we should take some of this to Captain Gamael?"

"Nope, he's the practical type," Karen said. "We need more to go on. And I think I know where to get it."

"You want me to go to the marketplace, have a knife thrown into my back, and then check it for fingerprints?"

"Not a bad idea, but we'll use it only as a last re-

60

sort," Karen said. She had taken her shoes off and was dumping the sand from them onto my bureau. "I want to follow someone."

"The guy with the green hat?"

"Uh-uh," she said. "Dr. Leonhardt."

By this time I knew enough about Karen to figure she hadn't flipped her lid. She had some way of following Dr. Leonhardt, I was sure. What it was, however, was something else again. She didn't say and I wasn't going to ask. By this time I knew something else about her. She liked to drop little hints like that so that I'd have to ask and she would look smart. This time I would be smart and just follow her lead.

"You think we can start this afternoon?" she asked.

"Sure, why not," I said.

"Good," she said, heading for the door. "I was wondering if you could make arrangements that quickly."

Out she went.

I locked the door behind her and sat by the window overlooking a nearly deserted street. It was still early afternoon and the sun was ferocious. A dog, one of the few I had seen in Egypt, sauntered lazily across the street. How in heaven's name, I asked myself, was I going to make arrangements for us to follow Dr. Leonhardt if I hadn't the slightest idea where he went. I hated to ask, and on the other hand I didn't want to have to face Karen and admit for the first time that I didn't know what she was talking about. I figured I might as well ask. I opened the door and took one step toward Karen's room when I was stopped in my tracks by the sight of a man kneeling in front of her door. He must have heard me because he jumped up and went quickly to the steps. I followed but by the time I got to the head of the stairwell the soft footfalls had faded away. I looked down the stairs just in time to see the top of a green hat disappear into the lobby.

I raced back to Karen's room and tried the door.

"Who is it?" she sounded okay.

"Me," I answered.

She opened the door with one hand as she held the other one up to let the nail polish dry.

"You shouldn't have opened the door," I said. "I didn't give my name."

"Only an American would say me," she said.

"Well, Green Hat was camped outside your door when I came into the hall," I said.

"That gives me the creeps," she said.

"Getting cold feet?" I asked hopefully. "After this morning and all?"

"Not yet," Karen said. "What do you say we hire Ahmed to take us around to all the places Dr. Leonhardt was digging and see what we come up with?"

"You have any idea how much that's going to cost? It can cost an arm and a leg!"

"I don't think so," she said. "And anyway, I'll use what money I have left. After all, I thought I was going to be here nearly a month."

"Okay—it's done!" I said, trying to work up some macho feelings.

"Of course if you don't want to go, it's all right," she said. "I might get killed or something and then you can feel rotten for the rest of your life."

I found Ahmed back at the theater and put the proposition to him. He was less than enthusiastic.

"You crazy! I don't go! I'm not crazy! Somebody might try to kill you and kill me instead. Go away!"

"How much did Dr. Leonhardt pay you a day?" I asked.

"Nothing, he left with my money," Ahmed said. "Now you leave, please."

"How much did Dr. Leonhardt promise you?" I asked, backing up the aisle of the empty theater. "I'll pay you."

"Go awaaay!" Ahmed put his hands over his eyes so he wouldn't see me.

"Aren't you interested in getting your money?" I asked.

"Forget the money," Ahmed said. "It's not worth running around in the desert for. I already ran around with your doctor. I don't want to go with you."

"All right, Ahmed," I said, turning to walk away. "I see I should be talking to Captain Gamael instead. Maybe he can find another driver for us."

I was almost to the front entrance when I heard Ahmed call me.

"My friend!" He put his hand on my arm. "Do you know how much money the doctor paid me?"

"No," I said.

"He paid me ten American dollars a day," Ahmed said. "You pay me double this?"

"Yes," I said.

"Oh, okay," Ahmed's face and shoulders dropped. "Then I take you around. When do you want to go?"

"How about meeting us back at the hotel in an hour?"

"Okay." There was real misery in Ahmed's black face. "I meet you in front of the hotel." He turned and walked away.

I guessed that twenty dollars a day was too much to resist, unhappy as he was at the prospect of joining Karen and me as targets.

At the hotel I finished a sandwich and watched as Karen negotiated with the waiter to get a large can of water. There was disappointment on her face when she got back to the table.

"Couldn't get the water?" I asked.

"Got the water," she said. She was spreading out a large sheet of paper on the table and putting condiment jars on its corners to hold it down.

"He wouldn't put ice in it?"

"Got the ice."

"Then what?"

"I like it with a little lemon. He only had lime."

"Pity. What's the paper?"

"What's it look like?"

"A map."

"I went back over Dr. Leonhardt's book. Starting from his first site I made this map, just using the directions he went in. He said he started digging at points A14 and then moved in an easterly direction."

"But he was writing about Tutankhamun's—" And then I saw what she was getting at, or thought I did. "You mean he said he was writing about his digs at Tutankhamun's tomb, but he really meant his exploration for Akhenaton."

"Hey, that's a good idea," Karen said. "We'll have to check that out later."

"Well what are *you* thinking?" I asked.

"I'm thinking that I hope Ahmed thinks that the map is legit so he just takes us to the places he and Dr. Leonhardt went to."

The girl made sense.

The jeep that Ahmed showed up in had a wooden canopy built over it. The outside was light blue and the inside black with a yellow moon and red and white stars.

"Art Tacko," Karen commented sweetly.

She took out the map she had made and examined it carefully just out of Ahmed's line of vision.

"Show me where you want to go," Ahmed said, leaning back to get a peek at the map.

"Just take us to the second place he was digging. We'll tell you where we want to go from there," Karen said, quickly folding the map and putting it under the seat.

Ahmed grunted and began to drive. He drove for about an hour through some of the most desolate land I had ever seen. Finally he stopped and pointed toward a small dune.

"There," he said.

He pulled the jeep to a stop. The wind had picked up and the sand cut into our faces. Ahmed lowered his hood and produced a scarf from somewhere which he handed to Karen. We walked slowly over to the dune, up to our shoe tops in the loose sand.

We looked around the site. There were no signs of digging at all. I went to the crest of the dune, or as near to it as I could to see if there was anything under it. Nothing. I looked off in the distance. The Nile was a half mile away. It was the part of the river that had overflowed when the Aswan dam was built and that had engulfed what little greenery there was. I could see a few patches of grass growing out of the silt deposits along the water's edge, and the remains of a Nubian village.

I looked around for a long while, tramping

through the sand, looking for any signs whatsoever of digging. I found none. The wind had died down, and I thought about the water that Karen had brought.

I got back to the jeep at the same time Ahmed and Karen returned from the other side of the dune.

"You see anything?" she said.

"Nothing," I said.

The next site was a good half hour's drive away. This time Ahmed stopped at a rock formation very close to the Nile. He showed us what he said was the exact spot in which Dr. Leonhardt had been digging. We drew a large circle around the spot, above twelve feet in diameter, and began to probe with sticks. There was one area that might have been dug up before, but we couldn't tell for sure. We pushed the sticks into the soft earth carefully, so as not to break anything we might find under the earth's surface.

"I don't think this is the place," Karen called back. "If Dr. Leonhardt had really dug here the ground should have been looser."

"Ahmed, why isn't the ground looser here if Dr. Leonhardt dug here as you say?" I asked.

"He don't dig," Ahmed said. "He never dig. He just push a stick into the ground, like you."

"In that case," Karen said, rubbing her nose. "He wasn't serious about digging here. Anything that he would have been interested in wouldn't be anywhere near enough to the surface to find with a probe. You would have to dig at least six to fourteen feet, depending on the amount of erosion in the area, before you could even think about using a probe."

"I don't think that Ahmed understands that," I said. "Better explain it to him carefully."

"Dr. Leonhardt's an Egyptologist," Karen said. "Anything he would be looking for would be either above the ground, like a pyramid, or many feet below the ground, covered by years of dirt blowing over it. You understand?"

"I understand," Ahmed said. "But that's what he did. Like I say."

We went around to two more sites where Ahmed said that Dr. Leonhardt had been digging. We didn't see any signs of digging at all.

"I think," Karen said as we got back into the jeep, "that we are being had by Mr. Ahmed. You, of course, noticed that we are traveling in a direction for which there is a constant equidistant point?"

"Huh?"

"We're traveling in a circle!" she said.

I asked Ahmed to stop the jeep and I got out. I couldn't see very much where I was, so I walked up to the base of a small hill and began climbing. When I had gone up about thirty feet, I looked around. Sure enough, there was the same deserted Nubian village I had seen before, but now I was looking at it from the other side. Either Ahmed was taking us for a ride or Dr. Leonhardt was taking everybody for a ride. I stood and waved toward Ahmed's jeep. Karen stuck her head out of the side and I beckoned again. She came out and started toward me.

"You find something?" she asked. There was a trickle of sweat running down the side of her face. Good, she sweats.

"No," I said, "but you were right about us going in a circle. I spotted that village over there from the first place Ahmed took us. How did you know?"

"I had this with me," she said, reaching into her blouse and pulling out a compass she had on a chain around her neck. "You think Ahmed is just running us around for the money?"

"On the one hand I think he is," I said. "On the other hand I'm not too sure."

"I'm glad you have only two hands."

"You know what I was thinking of when we probed around with those sticks?" I asked.

"A clam dig?"

"A clam dig? No, but that's what Dr. Leonhardt could have used those long knives and—"

The idea hit us both at the same time. All of the cooking utensils, the long handled spoons, the spatulas, the oversized forks, could have been used as digging tools.

"But if he was down to that level," Karen said,

"he must have finished digging or whatever he was investigating had to be above the ground."

"There's nothing around here, though," I said. "Or at least Ahmed pretends not to know of anything."

"You want to hear a wild hunch?" Karen asked.

"No, but go ahead."

"Sometimes you get a small monument that's looted, okay?"

"Go ahead."

"Then somebody sees it's empty and moves in."

"Go ahead," I said, wanting her to hurry and trying to figure out what she was going to say before she said it.

"Then some other people move near them and start a village."

"Like in Karnak," I said. "The Christians lived in the temples when the Romans ruled Egypt."

"Right, or maybe like your village over there."

"Doesn't make any sense," I said. "If it was the tomb of an Egyptian king it would either be in a pyramid or a mountain, like the Valley of the Kings. Still, Akhenaton's mother was a Nubian."

We both stood staring at the village.

"How many deserted Nubian villages are we ever going to get to see?" Karen said.

It was worth a try. I waved over to Ahmed who was leaning against a tree watching us, and pointed toward the village. He shrugged and we went down the mountain side.

"There's an old Nubian village over there," I said. "Let's go and take a look."

"That village is not Nubian," Ahmed said. "It's Egyptian."

That was a bit of a damper, but it didn't bother me as much as the uneasy feeling I had in the pit of my stomach. Karen told him that we wanted to see it anyway. Ahmed said it was getting late and we should start out in the morning.

"If you want to stay here we'll take the jeep and pick you up on the way back," Karen said.

Ahmed shrugged, got into the jeep, and we started for the village. It would be odd, I thought, to have an Egyptian village so far away from the main town of Aswan.

Ahmed didn't break any speed limits getting there. And he never stopped complaining.

"Sometimes there are wild animals in these places," Ahmed said.

"I doubt it," I said. I hadn't seen an animal that wasn't working since I reached Egypt.

"Just in case, though, " Ahmed said, "maybe we should stop here."

He stopped the jeep and folded his arms over his chest. We were about a hundred yards away from the village. It certainly looked deserted. Karen jumped out of the jeep and started for the village on foot. Ahmed threw both hands up to the sky, shook his head, and mumbled something about crazy Americans.

He started the jeep and quickly caught up with her.

"I take you," he said. "I blow the horn to scare away the animals."

She gave me this look as she got back into the jeep that said she thought she was at least the Queen of Sheba or somebody. She was actually a little taller sitting in the seat.

"Not bad," I said.

"It takes," she said, "a little nerve."

Thanks. I needed that. I slumped down in my seat as best I could as we proceeded slowly toward the village with Ahmed blowing the horn to scare away the animals. I started to make a joke about circling it three times and maybe the walls would fall, but thought better of it.

The village was a nest of dirt and stone houses. On the way to the market in Aswan I had seen two men building one of them. They were stacking rows of bricks they had made from mud and cementing them with a slightly different mixture of mud. The driver of the carriage we were in said that they sometimes lasted for two or three generations.

There were a number of domed buildings still standing and I imagined them to have been either meeting places or official buildings, and therefore, made stronger than the others. One thing I was sure of, they were Nubian buildings.

"I don't see anything here," Ahmed said, as we entered the village.

I saw, in the courtyard of one building, a painting on the wall. The color was mostly faded except for the top part which depicted a bright blue sky.

"When was this village deserted?" I asked Ahmed over the din of the horn.

"What?"

"When was this village deserted?" I was still shouting despite the fact that he had stopped the horn.

"When they built the dam," Ahmed said. "These people were moved to a safe place, but the dam didn't send the water this way."

We got out and started to walk around.

"They always have snakes in places like this," Ahmed called after us.

I did see something, but it wasn't a snake. I went after Karen as quickly as I could and whispered to her. She looked at me and then went back to the jeep quickly without saying a word. I thought that she finally was getting a little nervous and was ready to back down for a bit. I should have known better.

"John has found some tire tracks that look fresh," she said. "Someone's been using this place recently. Have *you* been here before?"

Ahmed just looked at her and started blowing the horn harder.

"I think all you did was to get him ticked off," I said.

"So what?" she said. "I'm not worried about him

getting ticked off. And his blowing that horn won't stop me from demanding an answer."

Ahmed stopped blowing the horn and started waving his hand. We turned in the direction that he was looking and saw two men coming toward us, one with a rifle.

Whatever was going on, we had found it. I knew the only chance we had was to grab the jeep and get out of there. I jumped into the front seat and yelled for Karen. She dove into the seat beside me.

Ahmed was caught by surprise, but not for long. He grabbed the steering wheel. Holding the wheel with my left hand for leverage, I sent a straight right to his jaw. It landed with a crunch and I could hear the sound of bones breaking.

"Why you do that?" Ahmed's voice came to me as I doubled over from the pain of my broken hand. "You should never strike a man's face. They do that kind of thing in your country?"

"Why do you bring them here? You are more stupid than a camel!"

Mr. Mahdou's voice was a shock. The owner of the Grand was dressed in a jellaba and obviously beside himself with rage. He had balled his hands into tight fists and was banging them on the fender of the jeep.

"What could I do?" Ahmed said. "They wanted to hire a car and have somebody bring them to where the professor was digging. They have a map.

I bring them here thinking maybe they don't see anything, but they see the tire marks."

I shot Karen a glance that would have been a lot meaner than it was if my eyes weren't filled with tears from the pain in my hand.

"Take them to the storeroom," Mr. Mahdou said to the guy with the rifle. "If they don't behave properly, shoot them both."

A moment later we were both being pushed through the village. I thought about running, but I could already feel the bullets in my back. I was so scared I could hardly bend my legs to walk and Ahmed kept pushing me.

We were taken into what looked like a storeroom that had been converted to a garage. There were shelves against one wall and a low bench against the other. There weren't any windows, but a shaft of light came from a hole in the domed roof. The room smelled of oil as if someone had used it to repair cars. At the far end there were large wooden doors. The wood at the bottom was newer than the rest of it. There was a car in the middle of the floor. It looked to be about ten years old. I glanced at the tires as Ahmed shoved me toward a corner. They were the ones that had made the tracks that the Mouth had been so eager to confront Ahmed with.

The guy who had the rifle gave it to Mr. Mahdou. He was a short guy, about as wide as he was tall, and bald except for a little knit cap that he wore.

He produced a rope from somewhere and, pushing me to the ground, tied my ankles and then tied my arms behind my back. My hand was throbbing with the pain. I heard a scuffing noise and figured that Karen was being tied up, too. She was sniffling.

Once we were tied up, the three of them left. I could hear the door slam and lock and Mr. Mahdou yelling at Ahmed as they left.

I didn't hear anything from Karen and I was half afraid to call out to her. I thought they had just tied her up, but when I didn't hear her I thought they might have done something else to her. Visions of assassins with knives they were only too willing to use came to me. Then I reasoned that if they had killed her, they would probably have killed me too. It wasn't the most comforting thought.

"Who's . . . who's there?" A gravely voice broke the stillness. It wasn't Karen's voice, I knew. I tried to turn my head but couldn't do much the way I was tied. There was light in the room which came in through the cracks in the heavy wooden door and the hole in the domed roof.

"John?" Karen's voice. "Was that you?"

"No," I whispered back.

"It's me," the gravely voice seemed to come from nowhere. "I am being held prisoner here."

"Who are you?" I called back in a low voice.

"My name is Erich Leonhardt," came the strained reply. "I'm an American."

"And you're also my great-uncle," I said. "I'm John Robie. Karen Lacey is here, too."

"I'm certainly sorry to meet you under these circumstances," he said.

"We're tied up," I said. "You have any ideas about how to get out of here?"

"You were my only hope," Dr. Leonhardt said. "Now it's all over."

"Don't say that," I said.

"It's true," he answered.

"I didn't say it wasn't true," I said, "I just asked you not to say it."

"My mouth's not gagged," Karen said.

"So what? You could scream your lungs out and nobody would hear you out here."

"I was thinking I could loosen your ropes with my teeth," she said. "Can you get to the front of the car?"

The movement brought some circulation back into my arms, which was a good thing. The pain returned with it. But I managed to get to my knees and half roll, half drag myself to the front of the car. Karen rolled, and soon she was pulling and tugging at my ropes.

When I got loose, my right hand was so swollen it was just about useless. I untied Karen's hands using my one good hand and my teeth. Once I got her hands free, she untied her legs and mine and then went to help Dr. Leonhardt. He was sitting on the floor in the front of the car with his hands tied to the steering wheel.

"Why didn't you blow the horn to attract attention?" Karen asked.

Dr. Leonhardt pressed the horn button in way of response. Nothing happened. Then he looked around the room until he spotted a tin can and went to it on unshaky legs. It was water.

We watched as he scooped handfuls of water out of the can. He looked terrible. There were several bruises on the side of his face, and the flesh hung from him as if someone had draped skin loosely on a skeleton.

"They beat you?" I asked.

"No, no," he said, licking his dried, cracked lips. "They only threatened to. They gave me just enough food to keep me alive, and enough water to make me beg for more. The bruises are from my efforts to escape."

"You're saying there's nothing we can do?" Karen said.

"I'm saying that there is nothing I have thought of," Dr. Leonhardt said. "I was hoping that you would get the clues I put in the letter they made me write to you, and contact the authorities."

"We did, in a way," I said. "First we noticed that Sibuna spelled backwards was Anubis."

"You did," Karen said as she carefully inspected the room we were in.

"The thing with the monuments came later. We figured you were somewhere around Aswan."

"Splendid, I thought you would be bright," Dr. Leonhardt said, "but why didn't you contact the authorities?"

"We did," Karen said. "Or at least Captain Gamael spoke to us. But I think Mr. Mahdou has him convinced that you just took off without paying your bill."

"Ironic, isn't it?" Dr. Leonhardt said, sitting on a wooden crate. "I spend most of my life trying to achieve a certain amount of recognition and then end up being known as a bill dodger."

"Don't give up yet," I said.

"How could I have been so wrong about Mr. Mahdou?" Dr. Leonhardt said. "I confided in the man. He was so sympathetic when the university cut off my funds. That's when I had to move to his hotel. I know the Grand has seen better days. Frankly, so have I. Mr. Mahdou asked me if I would allow him to finance my dig. I should have known better. Whenever there is an important archeological find in Egypt, the wolves come out of their dens sniffing for gold."

"When did you become suspicious of him?" Karen asked.

"When he practically forced Ahmed on me as an assistant and insisted that I tell no one but him what I was doing."

"Then you started trying to throw him off the track?"

"Exactly. I told him I had made a mistake," Dr. Leonhardt said. "I even made a big display of selling my digging tools."

"And you bought cooking utensils to replace them," I said.

"You knew this, too?" Dr. Leonhardt shook his head sadly. "You would have made wonderful archeologists."

"We *are* going to be," Karen said. "If we can get out of this mess."

"Brought about by my stupidity," Dr. Leonhardt said. "They planned to keep me here until I revealed the site that might have been the final resting place of Akhenaton. But even I knew that once I told them that they could do nothing but . . . dispose of me."

"Too bad this wasn't a real tomb," I said. "They used to put weapons in the tomb with the pharoahs so they could hunt on their journeys through the underworld."

"Yes, and sacred oils, too," Karen said. She was rubbing her nose with the flat of her hand.

"Let's hear it, Karen," I said. "You're thinking of something."

"Dr. Leonhardt said that they put the battery back into the car when they wanted to use it, right?"

"Go on."

"So there must be gas in the car. If we could get at it we could start a fire, maybe burn the door down and make a run for it."

"There's a tank over there. I think it's full of some sort of petrol," Dr. Leonhardt said.

I checked and found that it was full of gas. I thought we could soak some rags and wait for them to come back. If we could find a match we could light the rags as they came in the door, throw them at the kidnappers, and snatch the gun. Then I took a look around at what we had to work with. Karen was probably in the best shape of us all at the time. My hand was busted and so swollen I couldn't make a fist if I tried, and Dr. Leonhardt looked weak from hunger. Karen said she would give it a try, but even she didn't think it would work.

"Fighting them won't work," Dr. Leonhardt said, "but your idea is fairly sound. Let's see if we can find a match."

Dr. Leonhardt and I looked in every corner of the building. We found a few candles, a copy of a soccer magazine and an old newspaper, but no matches. Karen didn't look. I was going to ask her why she wasn't and then I saw that she was crying. I felt bad for her. Dr. Leonhardt was the first to give up, and I followed a close second.

"Did you try the glove compartment?" Karen asked.

There was not one, but two books of matches in the glove compartment.

"I figure they'll wait until it gets dark and then kill us," Karen said. "That way they can take us someplace and bury our bodies in the desert."

It *was* logical.

Dr. Leonhardt had a plan: We would soak a rag and put it in the mouth of the gasoline can. When they came to get us we would light it just before they came in. We would hide behind the car, and when they opened the door—poof!

But Karen thought it sounded risky.

"Because it's nighttime, we might not find our way back even if we do get away," she said. "The chances of us getting the jeep before one of us gets shot isn't too good either."

She was right. I didn't have any other ideas, though.

"We could try to send out a signal," Karen said. "If we could burn some of the gasoline near the crack in the door, someone might see the smoke."

"There might be an even better way," Dr. Leonhardt said.

Since he had been working on the problem of getting out with us he had begun to sound better. I could see that he looked a little like Mom around the eyes.

"You think we can get the smoke up through that hole?" Karen asked as Dr. Leonhardt looked up at the small hole in the middle of the dome.

"Believe me, these so-called 'primitive' places are ingeniously designed. That is not simply a hole, but an air vent that allows heat to escape. If we burn the fuel anywhere in here it will go out of that hole."

I pried off one of the hubcaps with a broken screwdriver. Karen tore my shirt up and poured the gasoline over it. Then we put it in the hubcap, put the magazine over it, and dumped as much water as the hubcap could hold over the whole thing so it wouldn't burn too quickly. We put it directly beneath the air vent and Dr. Leonhardt lit it. It blazed and then died down to a small flame, sending thick black smoke straight up. It smelled terrible. We put a sleeve that we had saved into the mouth of the can, making a huge Molotov cocktail. Then we waited.

We waited for what seemed a good half hour. The fire in the hubcap went out, and we had to get more gas from the can and start all over again. Finally we heard some shouts. Karen and I hid behind the car while Dr. Leonhardt stood with the gas can in front of the door. At the last moment, just as we heard the lock being turned, Dr. Leonhardt lit the rag that was in the mouth of the gasoline can and ran back behind the car with us.

The door swung open and the bald man with the rifle came in. He saw the rag burning in the gasoline can and snatched it out with his bare hand. He and Ahmed stamped it out and then took the gas can outside. Mr. Mahdou looked in cautiously. He said something in Arabic to Baldy, gave the rifle to

Ahmed, and went back to the small house they had come from.

"Ahmed!" I called out. "Look, you're a reasonable guy. Let us go, and we won't say anything about this to anyone."

I took a deep breath and stood up. Out of the corner of my eye I saw Karen stand, too.

"Besides," she said, "if you shoot us somebody might hear you. Sound really travels very . . . very . . ."

I saw what had stopped Karen in mid-sentence. Baldy had come back wielding the most wicked-looking dagger I had ever seen. They had thought about the noise, too.

"Look, I'll tell you where the tomb is," Dr. Leonhardt said, "just let the children go."

"Now it's too late," Mr. Mahdou said. "Now you make me a murderer."

I thought I heard myself screaming as I ran. I wasn't sure why I was screaming, maybe it was something about not wanting to hear the shots in case they did shoot at me. I had just got past Mr. Mahdou and Baldy was after me when I heard the shot. I must have tried to take too big a step, and the next thing I knew I was hurtling to the ground. The sand came up fast and I soon had a faceful of it. I could just about feel the knife in my back as I twisted around to face the man I knew would kill me. I couldn't see for the sand in my eyes and tried desperately to get it out, tearing at my undershirt with one hand and feeling out with the other to ward off the blows of the knife.

I finally got my eyes open wide enough to see that Baldy wasn't anywhere near me. I thought they might be going back to finish off Karen and Dr. Leonhardt first and then come after me. I got to my knees and tried to see what was going on.

"You all right, my friend?"

The voice came from behind me and I nearly jumped out of my skin as I twisted around. It was Captain Gamael. There were several policemen with him and one civilian.

"I think you've met Lieutenant Qassem?"

I hadn't met the lieutenant face to face, but I recognized the green hat.

I found Karen and Dr. Leonhardt still in the storeroom-turned-garage and went to them as Captain Gamael's men rounded up and handcuffed Mr. Mahdou, Ahmed and Baldy. Baldy was screaming in Arabic and spitting on the ground in Mr. Mahdou's direction.

"Did Green Ha—I mean, the lieutenant follow us out here?" I asked.

"He did but he couldn't get too near because it is all open," Captain Gamael said. "He radioed back for us. We thought you were lost in the desert until we saw your smoke signal. Very clever. I thought you two might lead us to the doctor."

"You mean all the time you thought there was something wrong beside Dr. Leonhardt just skipping out on the bill?" Karen asked.

"Precisely," Captain Gamael was playing with a bullet, turning it over in his thick fingers.

"When you young people came and read the letter which was supposed to be from Dr. Leonhardt, I already knew it had not come from Khartoum. You saw that I had Dr. Leonhardt's other mail, didn't you? I gave you plenty of time to look at it. I had instructed the post office to let me see all mail to or from Dr. Leonhardt. When Mr. Mahdou told me that you had received a letter from Leonhardt, a letter the post office knew nothing about, I began to wonder about his involvement.

"But I still didn't know where Dr. Leonhardt was. I couldn't prove anything definite about Mahdou either. So I asked Lieutenant Qassem to try to keep an eye on you. He saw that you were talking to Ahmed. After the incident in the market, we really started to watch the two of you. But you had already noticed that he was following you. So he had to follow from a greater distance. He almost lost you when you went into the desert with Ahmed. It was good we found you when we did. At first our friends just wanted to scare you away, but when you found them out . . ."

I turned and looked at Mr. Mahdou. He looked away from me, over the desert.

"The gold of the pharoahs," Mr. Mahdou spoke

without turning back. "It would have been enough to make me rich beyond my wildest dreams. My wildest dreams."

We watched as Captain Gamael's men herded Mr. Mahdou and his pals into the police van.

"If you two ever get tired of archeology, I can always use two good people on my force," Captain Gamael smiled.

"Not me," I said.

"What does it pay?" Karen asked.

Captain Gamael laughed. He assigned one of his men to drive us back to Aswan and waved to us from the front seat of the van as it made the turn back toward town.

"It's a funny thing," Dr. Leonhardt said. "I told Mr. Mahdou that I thought I might be able to find Akhenaton's mummy, and he just assumed there would be a treasure with it."

"I thought the ancient Egyptians buried their pharoahs with a great deal of treasure," Karen said.

"Akhenaton had fallen out of favor with the Egyptian royalty," Dr. Leonhardt said. "And either his tomb, like so many others, had already been robbed, or he was not buried in the same manner. Strangely enough, it was Akhenaton who believed in worshiping one supreme god. Yet today, thousands of years after his death, men still come to their ruin by worshiping gold. Akhenaton would definitely not have approved of Mr. Mahdou and his friends."

We moved to the Cataract Hotel that evening, and I was glad of it. Dr. Leonhardt didn't look half bad when he had cleaned himself up and shaved. In fact, he looked a little like I had expected him to. He made us go over each detail of what we had done since reaching Egypt, and I think he really enjoyed finding out how we had eventually found him. It was easy to see why he found pleasure in digging up the mysteries of ancient kingdoms.

By the next morning, the story was in the local papers and on the radio. We couldn't read the paper, which was in Egyptian, but the English broadcaster referred to me and Karen as Dr. Leonhardt's "two American assistants." By the afternoon the University of Chicago had offered to review Dr. Leonhardt's request for funding, and the Egyptian government had also offered him the staff to continue his search for Akhenaton's mummy.

"If I can secure the permission of your parents," Dr. Leonhardt said, looking over his glasses, "would you two be willing to spend a few more weeks with me? I can assure you they won't be as exciting as the week you've just had, but they might be more rewarding."

"I'd love to," Karen said.

"You mean to actually do some archeological work?" I asked.

"Precisely," Dr. Leonhardt said.

"I'd really dig that," I said.

Karen groaned and Dr. Leonhardt winced.

"In the meanwhile I can figure out how I can tell my folks what happened. First Dr. Leonhardt mysteriously disappeared, then there was this snake in Karen's bed. Then someone threw a dagger at us in the marketplace which wasn't half as scary as when we were captured by the kidnappers in this deserted Nubian village, see . . ."

"Let's just tell them that we didn't see Dr. Leonhardt at first, but then we looked around and found him," Karen said.

The girl was smart. She really was.

AK
F
Mye

Tales of a Dead King